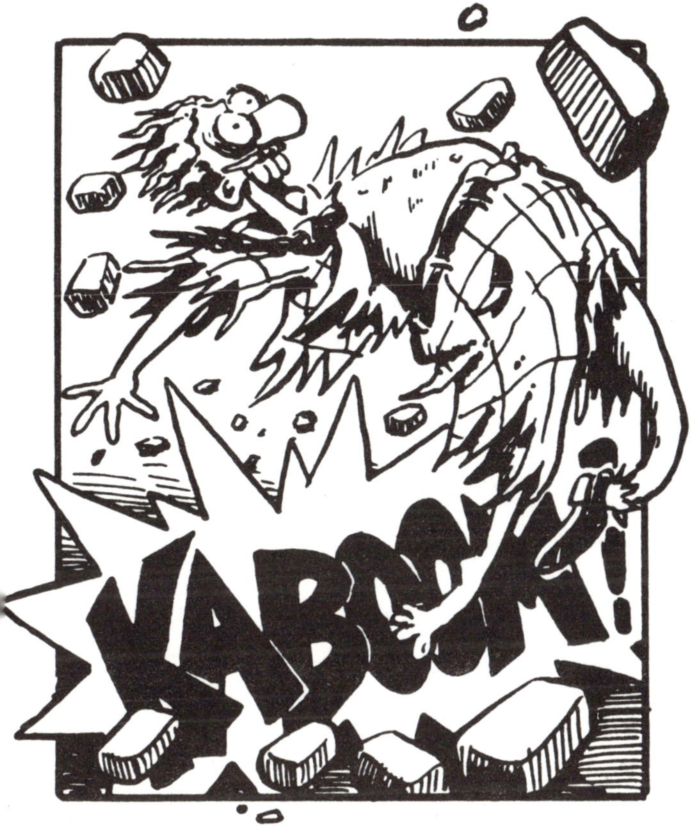
KABOOM!

TRUST ME!

ERNIE'S FIRST YEAR

By BUD GRACE

3^50

BG18

D1782764

A King Features COMIC

AVON BOOKS NEW YORK

TRUST ME! is an original publication of Avon Books. This work has never before appeared in book form.

AVON BOOKS
A Division of
The Hearst Corporation
105 Madison Avenue
New York, NY 10016

"A King Features Comic"
Copyright © 1990 by King Features Syndicate, Inc.
Published by arrangement with King Features Syndicate, Inc.
Library of Congress Catalog Card Number: 89-92472
ISBN: 0-380-76069-X

All rights reserved, which includes the right to reproduce this book or portions thereof in any form whatsoever except as provided by the U.S. Copyright Law. For information address Avon Books.

First Avon Books Trade Printing: February 1990

AVON TRADEMARK REG. U.S. PAT. OFF. AND IN OTHER COUNTRIES, MARCA REGISTRADA, HECHO EN U.S.A.

Printed in the U.S.A.

CW   10   9   8   7   6   5   4   3   2   1

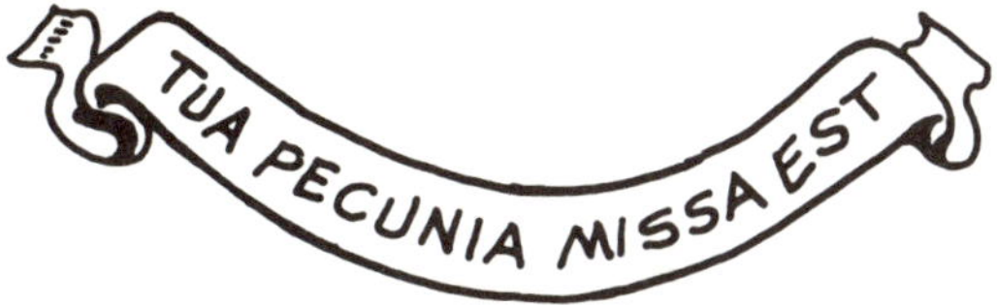
TUA PECUNIA MISSA EST

"The check is in the mail."

A super-slick bamboozler, a husband-hungry landlady, a virtuous wallflower and a 9-year-old hellion—improbable members of an even more improbable cast.

And yet anyone who has spent an evening with cartoonist Bud Grace knows these characters can exist. They are all extensions of Grace's slightly warped mind. How else would you describe the mind of a man who gave up a career in atomic physics to chart unexplored comic territory?

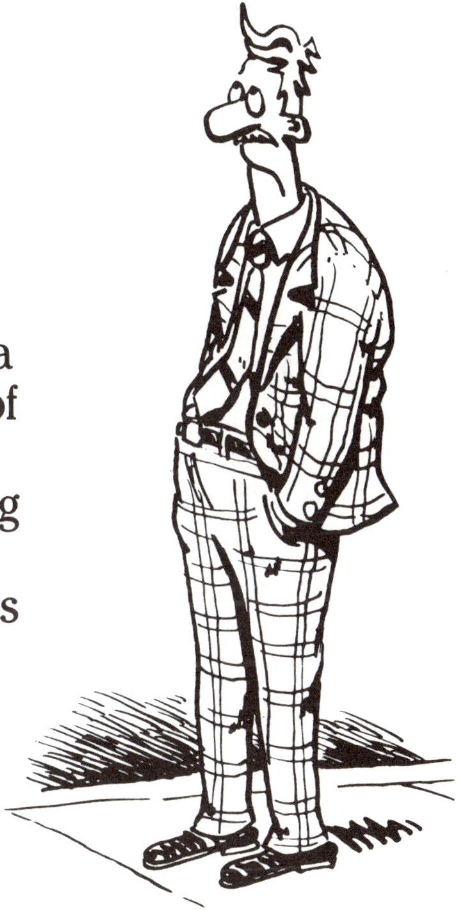

Bud Grace received his Ph.D. in physics from Florida State University. For nearly a decade, he taught and researched such topics as low energy neutral atomic scattering. In 1979, he quit to become a cartoonist, having never drawn before.

In 1988, his comic strip ERNIE debuted in papers across the country and hit a responsive funny bone in tens of thousands readers. So great has the response been that Piranha Clubs (read on and you'll understand) have formed around the world. They love him in Sweden!

So here are some of the strips from ERNIE's first year. Sit back and enjoy the lunacy.

THE APARTMENT

YOU DON'T HAVE ANY STRANGE HABITS, DO YOU? I DON'T WANT A WEIRDO ROOMMATE!
ROOM-MATE WANTED INQUIRE WITHIN
I KNOW WHAT YOU MEAN!
I HAD A REAL WHACKO ONCE - RAISED SNAKES! I'D GET DRESSED IN THE DARK AND END UP WITH AN ANACONDA AROUND MY NECK!-AND TALK ABOUT BLACKSNAKES!
I GOT SO BUMMED OUT I HAD TO GIVE UP THE CLARINET!
© 1988 King Features Syndicate, Inc. World rights reserved
THANK GOODNESS, MY CARNIVOROUS PLANTS KEPT THE NUMBERS DOWN
BOGRACE 2-23

I'M GLAD YOU'RE MOVING IN, UNCLE SID! TILL NOW, ALL I'VE HAD COME BY ARE WEIRDOS!
ROOM MATE WANTED INQUIRE WITHIN
THAT'S ONE THING YOU DON'T WANT-A WEIRDO ROOMMATE! TAKE IT FROM ME!
I'M WITH YOU 100% ON THAT!
WHAT COULD BE WORSE THAN LIVING WITH A LOONEY?
ABSOLUTELY NOTHING!
YOUR HALF OF THE RENT IS $175
I'LL GET IT FOR YOU NEXT WEEK, I SWEAR!
© 1988 King Features Syndicate, Inc. World rights reserved
Bo GRACE 2-24

NOW THAT WE'RE SHARING THIS APARTMENT, ERNIE, WE'RE BOTH GOING TO HAVE TO MAKE SOME ADJUSTMENTS IN OUR LIFE-STYLES
HEY! WHERE'S THE AFTER-SHAVE
AFTER-SHAVE? WHAT AFTER-SHAVE? WHO ARE YOU?
ME? I'M MARTY— HAROLD SAID I COULD MOVE IN
HAROLD?
HEY, RAOUL! WHAT KIND OF CRUMMY COMMUNE IS THIS IF YOU HAVE TO BUY YOUR OWN AFTER-SHAVE?
©1988 King Features Syndicate, Inc. World rights reserved
LIKE PRIVACY— WE MAY HAVE TO GIVE UP A LITTLE PRIVACY
RAOUL?
BARRE 2-25

I'D KNOCK FIRST, ERNIE- I RENTED MY HALF OF THE HALL CLOSET TO RAOUL FOR AN OFFICE.
GLOBAL ENTERPRISES CONGLOMERATE LTD. INC.
OH YEAH?! WELL, I'LL PUT AN END TO THIS! WHAT KIND OF BUSINESS CAN YOU RUN OUT OF A CLOSET, ANYWAY...
SHREEEEK
REND
TEAR
LACERATE
2-26
HE BREEDS DOBERMANS
SHAKE
QUIVER

YOU CAN'T DO IT, UNCLE SID! YOU CAN'T RENT YOUR ROOM OUT TO 28 PEOPLE!
I DON'T WANT TO GET NASTY, ERNIE, BUT I'VE GOT AN OFFICIAL DOCUMENT SIGNED BY THE GOVERNOR OF NEW JERSEY THAT SAYS I CAN
BO GRACE
© 1988 King Features Syndicate, Inc. World rights reserved
3-1
YOU TURNED MY APARTMENT INTO A STATE PRISON HALFWAY HOUSE?!
HEY! THESE GUYS NEED HELP!

LOOK, ERNIE, THIS PLACE IS HALF MINE, AND I CAN HAVE AS MANY ROOMMATES AS I WANT! THEY ALL SLEEP IN MY ROOM, THEY ALL SHARE MY HALF OF THE REFRIGERATOR, THEY ALL SHARE MY HALF OF THE CLOSETS...
OH YEAH?! DO THEY ALL SHARE YOUR HALF OF THE HOT WATER?! WHO'S GOING TO PAY FOR ALL THE HOT WATER?!
3-2
ANY OF YOU GUYS EVER TAKE A BATH?
NOPE
NOT ME
ARE YOU KIDDING?
NOOP
I HAD ONE IN '72
WHAT'S A BATH?
© 1988 King Features Syndicate, Inc. World rights reserved
ANY OTHER OBJECTIONS?
BOGRALE

THIS IS ELDRICH- MY NEW ROOMMATE. ELDRICH AND I WILL BE SPLITTING MY HALF OF THE RENT.
UH HUNNERT EIGHTEEN DOLLARS AN' SEVENNY-FIVE CENT UH MONTH! PERTY GOOD DEAL!
HEH HEH HEH
TICA TIKA TIKA
I CAN GET YOU IN FOR $6.27
©1988 King Features Syndicate, Inc. World rights reserved
BOORACE 3-3

I'VE HAD IT, UNCLE SID! I WANTED **ONE** ROOMMATE – YOU MOVED IN AND TURNED YOUR ROOM INTO A **KIBBUTZ**!
YOU DON'T LIKE US
IT'S NOT THAT
WHAT ABOUT **THEIR** FEELINGS, ERNIE? THESE GUYS ARE **LOSERS**! DO YOU KNOW WHAT IT FEELS LIKE TO BE REJECTED TIME AFTER TIME?
ESPECIALLY, BY SOMEONE THEY'VE GROWN TO LOVE AND RESPECT
© 1988 King Features Syndicate, Inc. World rights reserved
JUST GIVE ME ONE GOOD REASON WHY I SHOULDN'T MOVE OUT.
I'LL GIVE YOU 37 GOOD REASONS
OUR RENT WILL DOUBLE
3-4
BOBGRACE

THE BAR SCENE

WORLD'S TOUGHEST BAR

WORLD'S
TOUGHES
BAR
FREE PRETZELS!
THAT'LL BE EIGHT BUCKS
OUCH!
WHAT ABOUT PRETZELS?
HE'S DOING FIVE-TO-TEN FOR BREAKING A CUSTOMER'S ARM
2-4
BOGRACE

CAN I BUY YOU A BEER, MISS?
EER
SPLOOSH
EER
HEY! THE BEER'S WARM!
2·5 BOGRACE

FACE IT, ERNIE- THE DAYS OF CASUAL SEX ARE OVER!
I REMEMBER MY DAYS OF CASUAL SEX
BOTH OF THEM
© 1988 King Features Syndicate, Inc. World rights reserved
2-8

EXCUSE ME, YOUNG MAN, WOULD YOU PLEASE HELP ME ONTO THE STOOL?
NOW WHAT'S A SWEET LITTLE OLD LADY LIKE YOU DOING IN A TOUGH BAR LIKE THIS?
H'LO, EFFIE
FOUR FINGERS OF OLD CALCUTTA, HAFADOZEN EL ROPO CHEROOTS, A MEXICAN PIG'S FOOT AND LEAVE THE JAR!
B.GRACE
2-9
© 1988 King Features Syndicate, Inc. World rights reserved
Lunch

EVER BEEN TO DEETROIT? YOU LOOK JUST LIKE MY FOURTH HUSBAND! YOU GOT A "REMEMBER THE MAINE" TATTOO ON YOUR BACKSIDE?!
IS THAT A WIG?
YOU ARE! YOU'RE ALBERT GRUBOWSKI!! WEREN'T YOU DOING 20-TO-LIFE IN JOLIET?! WELL, YOU CAN'T HAVE ME BACK! I GOT REMARRIED...
MY NAME'S ERNIE FLOYD
PUFF SLURP
PUFF
SLURP
BOGRACE
© 1988 King Features Syndicate, Inc. World rights reserved
EIGHT TIMES
2-10

ERNIE FLOYD, MY FOOT! YOU'RE ALBERT GRUBOWSKI, MY FOURTH HUSBAND! DIDN'T THINK I'D KNOW YOU, DIDJA?
B. GRACE 2-11
WELL, I RECOGNIZE THOSE BEADY LITTLE EYES AND THAT WEEDY LITTLE MOUSTACHE! I REMEMBER THAT NONEXISTENT CHIN, THOSE THIN QUIVERING LIPS, THOSE STUPID...
OOPS!
KLUNK!
THOSE STUPID BONY ANKLES

YOU'RE ALBERT GRUBOWSKI, MY FOURTH HUSBAND AND I CAN PROVE IT!
LET'S SEE THAT TATTOO!
I SWEAR, LADY, I'M ERNIE FLOYD!
B. GRACE
I HOPE YOU'RE SATISFIED!
YES, WILFRED
2-12
WILFRED?
WILFRED POTTS, MY SIXTH HUSBAND...
I RECOGNIZED THE MOLE
AD
© 1988 King Features Syndicate, Inc. World rights reserved

THAT'S EIGHT SHOTS OF GIN, SIX EL ROPOS, FIVE BAGS OF JALAPEÑO PORK RINDS, AND - 4... 6... 8... SEVENTEEN PIG'S FEET
GIVE IT TO MY DATE
I'M NOT HER DATE!
B. GRACE
I DON'T HAVE TO GO HOME WITH HER, DO I?
2-13

MOVING IN

SID'S
RENT-A-HEAP
$5 DAY

THE LAST APARTMENT AD IN "THE TATTLER"... WHY DO I HAVE THIS AWFUL FOREBODING OF IMPENDING DOOM?
APT 4 RENT
WHY IS MY HEAD WHIRLING WITH DREADED VISIONS OF DÉJÀ VU?
C'MON, ERNIE! NOTHING COULD BE WORSE THAN SHARING AN APARTMENT WITH UNCLE SID AND HIS FORTY-THREE PAROLEES
APT 4 RENT
BOB GRACE
©1988 King Features Syndicate, Inc. World rights reserved
I'M NOT SURE, EARLENE, BUT I THINK IT'S MY DEAD AUNT WINONA'S BROTHER-IN-LAW!
APT 4 RENT
3-5

YOU CAN TELL MOHANDAS, GUNGA AND THE DORFMAN TWINS ADIOS! I GOT A NEW APARTMENT, AND I'M MOVING IN JUST AS SOON AS I CAN RENT A TRUCK!
3-7
YOU'VE CHEATED ME FOR THE LAST TIME, UNCLE SID!
SID'S
RENT-A-HEAP
$5 DAY
IS IT AIR-CONDITIONED?
© 1988 King Features Syndicate, Inc. World rights reserved

I DON'T KNOW, UNCLE SID- ARE YOU SURE THIS TRUCK CAN MAKE IT ALL THE WAY ACROSS TOWN?
SID'S RENT -A- HEAP
ARE YOU KIDDING?! IT'S ALREADY BEEN TO CALIFORNIA AND BACK SEVEN OR EIGHT HUNDRED TIMES!
3-8
SID'S RENT-A-
© 1988 King Features Syndicate, Inc. World rights reserved
HOW 'BOUT THEM RACING SLICKS!
BOB RACE

YOU'RE MAKING A SMART MOVE, ERNIE! THERE'S NO SENSE IN THROWING AWAY A LOT OF DOUGH RENTING A BRAND-NEW TRUCK!
TIKA TICKA TAKA
KACHUNK KACHUNK
TRUCK RENTAL (1 day @ $5) . . $5.00
SECURITY DEPOSIT $50.00
COLLISION INSURANCE $6.98
UNINSURED MOTORIST . . . $5.98
WIND-DAMAGE INSURANCE . $4.98
MALPRACTICE INSURANCE . $12.98
THAT'S IN CASE YOU SUE ME
OPTIONS:
CB RADIO $9.98
CB RADIO ANTENNA . $ 1.98
FUZZ BUSTER . . . $12.98
FIRE EXTINGUISHER . $14.98
TRAFFIC FLARES . . . $9.98
REAR-VIEW MIRROR . $13.98
SPARE TIRE $17.98
3-9
THE SPARE TIRE IS AN OPTION?!
YOU BETTER TAKE IT - THE LEFT REAR ON THAT SUCKER'S BALD AS A BABY'S BACKSIDE!

NO PROBLEM, ERNIE- I'LL HELP YOU PUSH-START IT
WR-RR-RR-RR-RR
WR-RR-RR-RR
SID'S RENT-A-HEAP
DRIP DRIP
SID'S RENT-A-HE AP
GRUNT
SID'S RENT-A-HE AP
BOGRACE 3-10
THAT OLD WRECK IN THE ALLEY IS FINALLY GONE-
I PAID SOME GUY NAMED SID 20 BUCKS TO HAUL IT AWAY

SO, I'M SORRY YOU HAD TROUBLE WITH THE TRUCK! WHAT DO YOU EXPECT FOR EIGHTY-NINE BUCKS?
SID'S RENT-A-HEAP
THINK OF THE MONEY YOU SAVED ON GAS
I HAD TO PUSH THIS WRECK EIGHTEEN BLOCKS
AND AS SOON AS HE PUSHES IT BACK, I'LL RETURN HIS DEPOSIT
© 1988 King Features Syndicate, Inc. World rights reserved
3-11

SID'S BIG PLAY

EFFIE MUNYON, MEET MY UNCLE SID
WHO ARE YOU?
ERNIE FLOYD, REMEMBER?-I RENTED YOUR APARTMENT YES-TERDAY. $350 A MONTH-I PAID YOU FIRST AND
LAST MONTHS' RENT. $700, REMEMBER?-I GAVE YOU $250 DAMAGE DEPOSIT?... $75 UTILITIES DEPOSIT?... I GAVE YOU $1025? CASH? YOU PUT IT IN YOUR COOKIE JAR?
HORACE PUTFARKIN, YOU OL' SHEIK! I'D KNOW YOU ANYWHERE! WHO ELSE DROOLS, EATS LIT CIGARS AND WEARS ELECTRIC UNDERWEAR!
BOGRACE 3-12

IT'S FATE WE MET, EFFIE! YOU KNOW AS WELL AS I THAT THE FUTURE HOLDS THE SAME THING IN STORE FOR US! WE CAN RUN FROM IT, BUT WE CAN'T HIDE! ESPECIALLY YOU...
NOW THAT YOU'RE IN YOUR SUNSET YEARS, FACE IT - YOUR TIME IS RUNNING OUT! WHEN A MAN COMES ALONG WITH A GOOD PROPOSAL, YOU GOT TO GRAB IT!
KNOW WHAT I MEAN?
YES, HORACE
MY NAME IS SID
I'LL MARRY YOU!
WHAT MARRY?! I'M TRYING TO SELL YOU A CEMETERY PLOT!!
© 1988 King Features Syndicate, Inc. World rights reserved
3-15
B. GRACE

CHORM
CHORMP
CHUMP
© 1988 King Features Syndicate, Inc. World rights reserved
CHORF
NORF
3-18
YOWLMP
THEY CALL IT PIEDS DES COCHONS VINAIGRETTE AND CHARGE $14.95!
CHORM
CHUMP
CHOMP
B.GRACE

IF YOU'LL EXCUSE ME, EFFIE, I HAVE TO GO TO THE LITTLE BOY'S ROOM...
CHOMP
CHUMP
CHUNK
CHURF
© 1988 King Features Syndicate, Inc. World rights reserved
I'LL JUST TAKE MY HAT ALONG-I ALWAYS WEAR MY HAT IN THE BATHROOM... AND MY UMBRELLA...
IN CASE A PIPE SPRINGS A LEAK
YOWLMP
EXIT
YEAH, I EAT IN SO MANY DIFFERENT RESTAURANTS. SOMETIMES I LOSE TRACK OF WHERE I'VE ALREADY BEEN
SNORK
B. GRACE 3-19

THE WEDDING ALBUM

OUR WEDDING
VOL VI
VOL VI

NOW WILL YOU FINALLY ADMIT THAT I'M NOT WILFRED POTTS?
2-15
B. GRACE
OUR WEDDING VOL VI
© 1988 King Features Syndicate. Inc World rights reserved
MAYBE YOU ARE, MAYBE NOT... BUT YOU'RE SURE NOT MY SIXTH HUSBAND
WHO WAS..?
FRANK PERDUE
THE CHICKEN CZAR?
OUR WEDDING VOL VI
I'D HAVE THOUGHT YOU'D REMEMBER SOMETHING LIKE THAT
IT'S ALL COMING BACK... OUR WEDDING NIGHT... HE WANTED ME TO FLAP MY ARMS AND SQUAWK LIKE A CHICKEN

MY THIRD HUSBAND, GOMEZ... BRILLIANT WRITER ... WE'D STILL BE MARRIED TODAY IF IT WEREN'T FOR THE ACCIDENT
OUR WEDDING VOL III
VOL III
HE WAS WORKING LATE... IT WAS AN EPIC ROMANTIC TRILOGY ABOUT A BEAUTIFUL YOUNG ACTRESS AND THE CREW OF THE USS SARATOGA
VOL III
SNURF
HIS TONGUE GOT STUCK IN THE TYPEWRITER AND HE BEAT HIS BRAINS OUT TRYING TO TYPE 'HELP'
BOB RACE 2-16
© 1988 King Features Syndicate, Inc. World rights reserved

IT'S TRUE, MRS. MUNYON- YOU REALLY HAVE BEEN MARRIED TWELVE TIMES! ARE YOU MARRIED NOW?
I'M NOT SURE - I THINK THERE'S SOMEBODY LIVING WITH ME, BUT I CAN'T REMEMBER WHO IT IS
ACTUALLY, SHE DOES LOOK A LOT LIKE MY FIFTH HUSBAND
©1988 King Features Syndicate, Inc. World rights reserved
2-17

THERE'S SOMETHING DIFFERENT ABOUT YOU, MRS. MUNYON
I CAN'T PUT MY FINGER ON IT
© 1988 King Features Syndicate, Inc. World rights reserved
GLUP GLURP
THAT'S IT! TEETH! YOU GOT TEETH!
I GOT TO PUT THEM **SOMEPLACE** WHILE THE GLASS IS BEING USED
B. GRACE 2-18

WOULD YOU EXCUSE ME WHILE I SLIP INTO SOMETHING MORE COMFORTABLE?
DON'T GO TO ANY TROUBLE, MRS. MUNYON, I GOT TO GO NOW, ANYWAY, SO I'LL JUST SAY GOOD NIGHT....
WHEN I WAS MARRIED TO FRANK PERDUE - HE GAVE ME THIS NEGLIGEE ON OUR HONEYMOON ~ USED TO DRIVE HIM CRAZY...
TUG
© 1988 King Features Syndicate, Inc. World rights reserved
BOGRACE
2-19

SO, MRS. MUNYON, YOU'VE BEEN MARRIED 10 OR 12 TIMES, BUT YOU'RE NOT SURE IF YOU'RE MARRIED NOW?
YES
YOU'RE ASKING?
EXCUSE ME, I HAVE TO MAKE A PHONE CALL.
B. GRACE
GUESS WHAT, EARLENE, SOME BOZO JUST PRO-POSED – NO, I DON'T KNOW HIS NAME, BUT HE LOOKS LIKE DON AMECHE
2-20
© 1988 King Features Syndicate, Inc. World rights reserved

THE BLIND DATE

TODAY'S YOUR LUCKY DAY, ERNIE! I GOT YOU A **BLIND DATE**!
GEE, I DON'T KNOW, UNCLE SID... IS SHE GOOD-LOOKING?
GORGEOUS! BEAUTIFUL! SHE MAKES VERA FUNK LOOK LIKE BRODERICK CRAWFORD!
WHO'S VERA FUNK?
BESIDES THAT, HER OLD MAN IS **LOADED**!
BALONEY!
NO LIE!! HE PAID ME A C-NOTE JUST TO GET HER A DA...
3-21
AHA!
OOPS
© 1988 King Features Syndicate, Inc. World rights reserved

FORGET IT! I'M NOT GOING ON ANY BLIND DATE! AT LEAST, NOT TILL I SEE A PICTURE!
OK! OK! I'LL GET YOU A PICTURE! I'LL GET YOU TEN PICTURES!
BEAUTIFUL HAIR, HUH?
YEAH, BEAUTIFUL.
THIS ONE, TOO- BEAUTIFUL HAIR... YEAH... YEAH...
DID YOU GET ANY OF THE FRONT OF HER HEAD?
© 1988 King Features Syndicate, Inc. World rights reserved
3-22
B. GRACE

I'VE GOT A BLIND DATE WITH DORIS HUSSELMEYER— YOU'RE NOT HERE TO SEE HER, TOO, ARE YOU?
DING DONG!
HECK, NO! I GOT A DATE WITH THE GOOD-LOOKING SISTER!
SHAKE A LEG, EUNICE!
© 1988 King Features Syndicate, Inc. World rights reserved
3-23

DORIS HUSSELMEYER? MY NAME'S ERNIE FLOYD- I BELIEVE WE HAVE A DATE TO GO BOWLING
NICE DRESS
I TAKE IT YOU'RE NEW AT THIS
AREN'T YOU SUPPOSED TO GIVE ME A WRIST CORSAGE OR SOMETHING?
© 1988 King Features Syndicate, Inc. World rights reserved
BS GRACE
3-24

NOW WHAT?
IF YOU'VE NEVER BEEN BOWLING BEFORE, HOW COME YOU OWN A BOWLING BALL?
I BOUGHT IT THIS MORNING
YOU BOUGHT A BOWLING BALL FOR A BLIND DATE ?!!
© 1988 King Features Syndicate, Inc. World rights reserved
3-25
I WANTED YOU TO LIKE ME
BOGRACE

ꓮZZIꓒ S'Ǝ
DO YOU BELIEVE IN LOVE AT FIRST SIGHT?
3-28
WELL, I-UHHHH... ACTUALLY, I ER... THAT IS, I REALLY DON'T, THAT IS, I...
I DO!
I THINK SOME PEOPLE ARE MEANT FOR EACH OTHER-LIKE HEPBURN AND TRACY, BOGART AND BACALL, JIM AND TAMMY...
fidget
WHO GETS THE ANCHOVY TRIPLE GARLIC?
B. GRACE

GEE WHIZ! WHERE DOES THE TIME GO?!! HERE IT IS NEARLY NINE O'CLOCK!! GOSH, I HAD A TERRIFIC TIME! GOT TO GET UP EARLY TOMORR...
3-29
© 1988 King Features Syndicate, Inc. World rights reserved
WELL, I'LL JUST SAY GOOD NIGHT! I-UHHH... I CAN TELL YOU'RE NOT THE KIND OF GIRL WHO KISSES ON THE FIRST DATE!
OH, DEFINITELY NOT! I PROMISED MY MOTHER I'D NEVER KISS ON THE FIRST DATE! NOT ME! I'M NOT THAT KIND OF GIRL!
WHEW
NO WAY
I WAS HER SECOND DATE... HER FIRST DATE WAS 1976 WITH SOME GUY FROM BRAZIL NAMED CLAUDE 'EL CHICO' ROMERO
RATTLE
BOGRACE

THANKS A LOT, UNCLE SID! THAT BLIND DATE YOU GOT ME TOOK ONE LOOK AND FELL MADLY IN LOVE! YOU GOT TO GET ME OUT OF THIS MESS!
DON'T LOOK AT ME, ERNIE! AND IF YOU'RE HER FIRST DATE IN TEN YEARS, IT'S NOT LIKELY SOME OTHER SAP IS GOING TO SHOW UP AND SWEEP HER OFF HER FEET!
I WAS SO EMBARRASSED! SHE EVEN INSISTED ON PAYING FOR DINNER.
© 1988 King Features Syndicate, Inc. World rights reserved
BUD GRACE 3-30

BUDDING ROMANCE

DORIS HUSSELMEYER IS TAKING ME TO THE GOLDEN MACKEREL FOR DINNER TONIGHT
THAT'S A PROBLEM?
DON'T YOU UNDERSTAND?! ONCE A WOMAN DECIDES YOU'RE THE ONE, IT'S AS GOOD AS OVER!! YOU'RE DEAD MEAT!! YOU MIGHT AS WELL RENT A TUXEDO!!
BOGRACE 4-1
IT'S LIKE THEY'RE PICKING OUT A LOBSTER FOR DINNER AT A RESTAURANT
NO, THE OTHER ONE- THE ONE WITH THE HEAD THAT LOOKS LIKE A ZUCCHINI WITH A HANDLE!
© 1988 King Features Syndicate, Inc. World rights reserved

DORIS HUSSELMEYER THINKS WE'RE GOING TOGETHER - TODAY SHE CLEANED MY APARTMENT
THAT DON'T MEAN NOTHING
IT'S FEMALE INSTINCT - THEY CAN'T HELP IT! IT'S THE YIN AND THE YANG— MEN ARE FILTHY, WOMEN ARE CLEAN! SHE DIDN'T CLEAN YOUR APARTMENT BECAUSE SHE'S GOT YOU HOOKED....
SHE HAD TO CLEAN IT - IT'S IN HER GENES
SHE HAD TO CLEAN IT - WE'RE GIVING A TUPPERWARE PARTY
3-31
BOGRACE

GADZOOKS! 'TIS DORIS... METHINKS I NEED A DISGUISE!
METHINKS YOU NEED A LOBOTOMY
© 1988 King Features Syndicate, Inc. World rights reserved
FORSOOTH! I SHALL RETURN ANUN!
ANON... YOU SHALL RETURN ANON.
4-4
BOGRACE

THE BEST WAY TO DUMP A BROAD IS TURN INTO A BUM! GET DRUNK—DON'T SHAVE—WATCH TV ALL DAY—DON'T CHANGE YOUR UNDERWEAR FOR A WEEK...
IT ALWAYS WORKED FOR ME
C'MON IN, DORISH GRAB A BEER
GREEN ACRES IS THE PLACE FOR ME
YOU NEED ME
BOB RACE
4-2
© 1988 King Features Syndicate, Inc. World rights reserved

DORIS KEEPS BUGGING ME TO TAKE HER TO A MOVIE
YOU WANT TO GET RID OF DORIS? TAKE HER TO A GOOD DOUBLE FEATURE
ENTERTAINMENT
© 1988 King Features Syndicate, Inc. World rights reserved
" DEATH SCREAMS OF THE MUTILATED CHEERLEADERS" AND "PSYCHOPATHIC BRAIN EATERS DO DALLAS"
IT JUST MIGHT WORK!
ENTERTAINMENT
HEH! HEH! HEH! ARRRGH!
OOO! OOO! I CAN'T LOOK! OOO!
OOO!
BGRACE 6-9

MEN DON'T MAKE PASSES AT GIRLS WHO WEAR GLASSES
TONIGHT'S THE NIGHT! I'LL BE SO GORGEOUS HE WON'T BE ABLE TO TAKE HIS EYES OFF ME!
ERNIE FLOYD- PREPARE TO MEET THY FATE!
4-6
DOES THIS BUS STOP AT 13th STREET?!

THE ALL-SEEING EYE SHOWS ME A TALL MAN WITH A HEAD THAT LOOKS LIKE A ZUCCHINI WITH A HANDLE!..
THAT COULDN'T BE ERNIE! ERNIE IS VERY, VERY HANDSOME!
ARE YOU ALMOST FINISHED? I WANT TO GO BOWLING
THE ALL-SEEING EYE TELLS ME YOU ARE VERY DEEPLY IN LOVE...
4-7
BROWNE

WHEN ARE YOU GOING TO SAY THOSE THREE LITTLE WORDS, ERNIE?
YOU KNOW I LOVE YOU, ERNIE! DON'T YOU LOVE ME?
SAY IT, ERNIE! SAY YOU LOVE ME!
WHAT DID YOU DO THEN?
WHAT ANY FAST-THINKING MAN WOULD DO— I DROVE MY CAR INTO A TREE
4-8
BUD GRACE

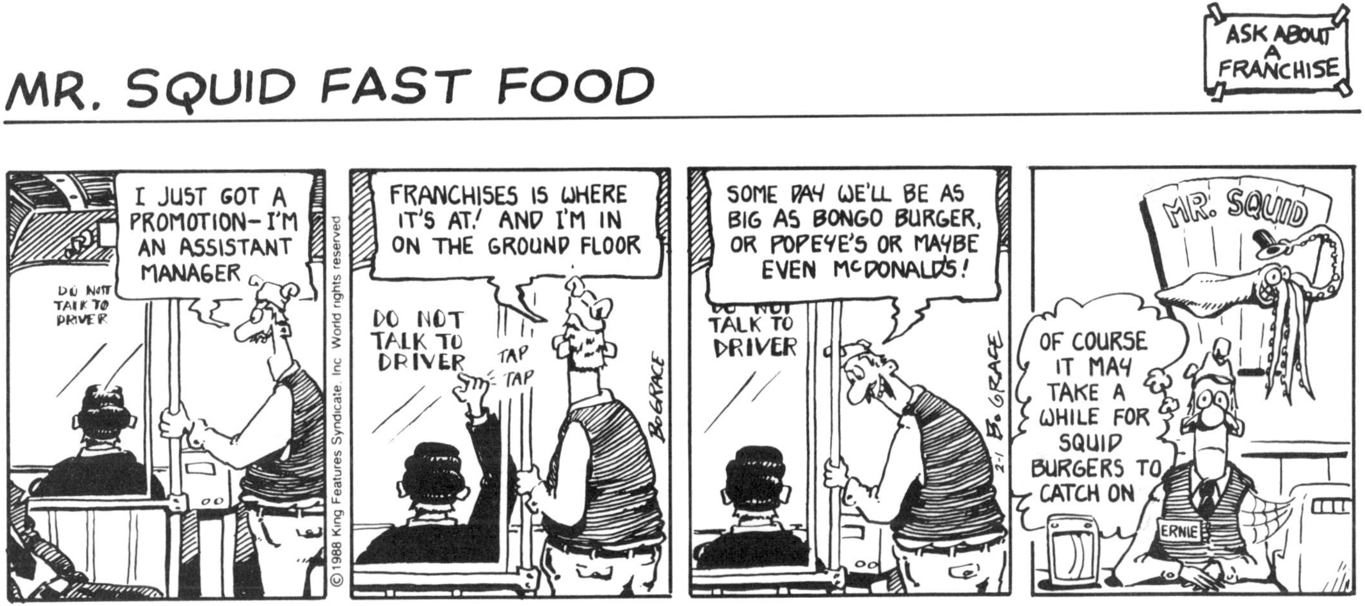
MR. SQUID FAST FOOD
ASK ABOUT A FRANCHISE
DO NOT TALK TO DRIVER
I JUST GOT A PROMOTION—I'M AN ASSISTANT MANAGER
© 1988 King Features Syndicate, Inc. World rights reserved
DO NOT TALK TO DRIVER
TAP TAP
FRANCHISES IS WHERE IT'S AT! AND I'M IN ON THE GROUND FLOOR
BO GRACE
TALK TO DRIVER
SOME DAY WE'LL BE AS BIG AS BONGO BURGER, OR POPEYE'S OR MAYBE EVEN McDONALD'S!
2-1 BO GRACE
MR. SQUID
OF COURSE IT MAY TAKE A WHILE FOR SQUID BURGERS TO CATCH ON
ERNIE

MR. SQUID
ASK ABOUT A FRANCHISE
THAT'S 4 SQUID BURGERS, 6 SQUID KABOBS, 2 BOXES OF SQUID NUGGETS, 4 SQUID HOAGIES, 4 SQUID CANOLIS, AND A GALLON OF ROOT BEER
MR. SQUID
ENJOY!
YOU BET I WILL!
ERNIE
IF THIS SLOP TASTES AS BAD AS IT LOOKS, MY IN-LAWS'LL BE GONE IN TWO DAYS MAX
ERNIE
BOGDACE 2-2
© 1988 King Features Syndicate, Inc. World rights reserved

I'LL HAVE THE SQUID THERMIDOR AVEC LES POMMES FRITES AND TENTACLES AU GRATIN
MY COMPLIMENTS, SIR, ON A VERY INTELLIGENT SELECTION
SNIFF
MR. SQUID
FRANCHISES AVAILABLE
WHILE YOU'RE AT IT, THROW IN A COUPLE OF THEM FRANCHEESIES
MR. SQUID
BO GRACE
2-3
© 1988 King Features Syndicate, Inc. World rights reserved

...FRANKLY, MR. MURRAY, NO ONE KNOWS THE FAST SQUID FOOD BUSINESS BETTER THAN ME...
CAL A. MURRAY, PRES.
IN SHORT, I DEMAND A POSITION COMMENSURATE WITH MY EDUCATIONAL BACKGROUND AND MY EXECUTIVE ABILITIES!
PERHAPS I'VE MISJUDGED YOU, MR. FLOYD... COME TO WORK TOMORROW WITH AN **ATTACHE CASE**!
CAL A. MURRAY, PRES.
DID YOU ORDER THE MUSHROOM DOUBLE SQUID OR THE SQUID KABOB SPECIAL?
MR. SQUID
WE DELIVER
© 1988 King Features Syndicate, Inc. World rights reserved

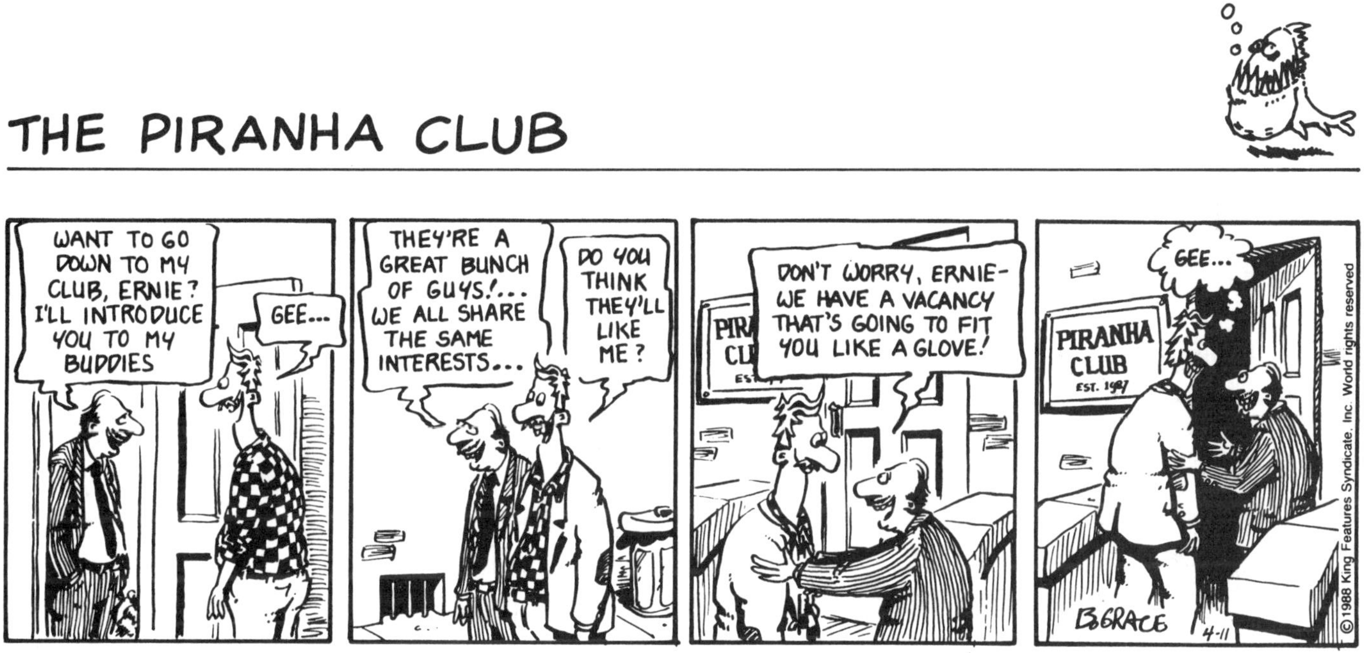
THE PIRANHA CLUB
WANT TO GO DOWN TO MY CLUB, ERNIE? I'LL INTRODUCE YOU TO MY BUDDIES
GEE...
THEY'RE A GREAT BUNCH OF GUYS!... WE ALL SHARE THE SAME INTERESTS...
DO YOU THINK THEY'LL LIKE ME?
DON'T WORRY, ERNIE- WE HAVE A VACANCY THAT'S GOING TO FIT YOU LIKE A GLOVE!
PIRANHA CLUB EST. 1987
GEE...
BGRACE
4-11
© 1988 King Features Syndicate, Inc. World rights reserved

WILLIE, MEET MY NEPHEW ERNIE FLOYD
PIRANHA CLUB
SQUEEZE
WHY DON'T YOU CALL OVER THE OTHER GUYS TO MEET ERNIE—
SURE, SID
PIRANHA CLUB
FEEDING FRENZY!
PIRANHA CLUB
WHAT A KIDDER!
WANNA BUY SOME ALUMINUM SIDING?
4-12
© 1988 King Features Syndicate, Inc. World rights reserved

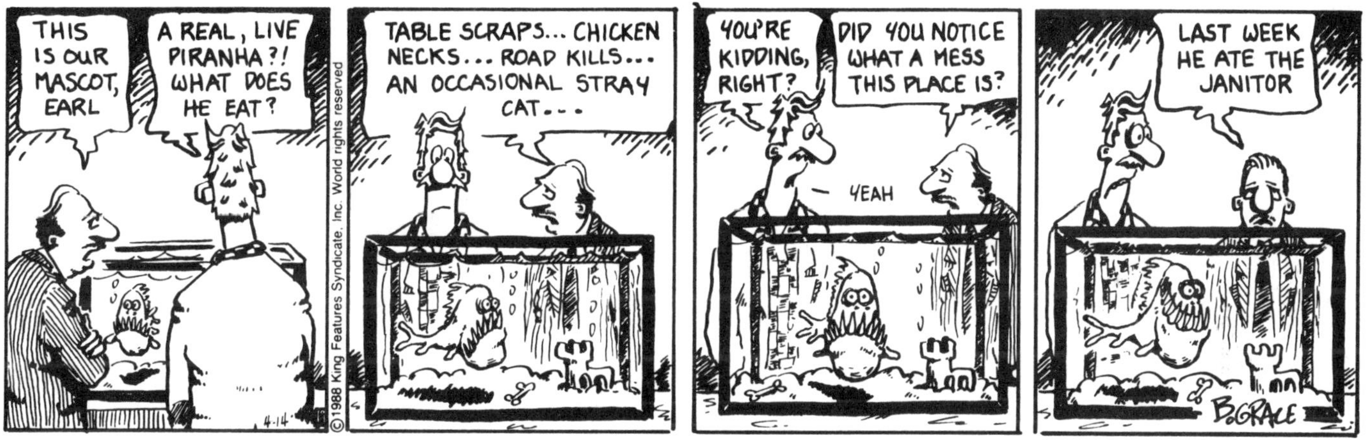
THIS IS OUR MASCOT, EARL
A REAL, LIVE PIRANHA?! WHAT DOES HE EAT?
4·14
©1988 King Features Syndicate, Inc. World rights reserved
TABLE SCRAPS... CHICKEN NECKS... ROAD KILLS... AN OCCASIONAL STRAY CAT...
YOU'RE KIDDING, RIGHT?
YEAH
DID YOU NOTICE WHAT A MESS THIS PLACE IS?
LAST WEEK HE ATE THE JANITOR
B. GRACE

I DIDN'T THINK IT WAS LEGAL TO OWN A PIRANHA
IT IS IF THEY'RE NEUTERED
WHO NEUTERED HIM?
WHAT'S HIS NAME—THAT VET OVER ON 12th STREET
'TWO FINGERS' MALONE?
YEAH
4-15

HOW COME PIRANHAS HAVE SUCH FLAT FACES?
4-16
© 1988 King Features Syndicate, Inc. World rights reserved
WIGGLE WIGGLE
WHAM!
ZIP!
BUD GRACE

JUST LIKE THE LIONS CLUB HAS AN EYE BANK AND THE SHRINERS HAVE A HOSPITAL, THE PIRANHA CLUB HELPS DISADVANTAGED YOUNG PEOPLE!
THAT'S NICE
EVERY YEAR WE RAISE MONEY TO HELP SOME POOR, DEPRIVED YOUNG PEOPLE EARN A LIVING!
HOW POOR ARE THEY?
ERNIE! THEY HARDLY HAVE ENOUGH CLOTHES TO WEAR!
HOW MUCH?

YOU JUST HAD YOUR ANNUAL PIRANHA CLUB FUND-RAISER LAST WEEK!
I WOULDN'T ASK YOU IF IT WASN'T A SPECIAL EMERGENCY!
9-19 BGRACE
WE WANT TO GIVE A PARTY FOR A CRIPPLED ORPHAN...
HOW MUCH?
HE DOESN'T HAVE A REAL LONG TIME TO LIVE, ERNIE!
© 1988 King Features Syndicate, Inc. World rights reserved
SO HOW LONG HAVE YOUR PARENTS BEEN DEAD, HERB?
OH— 50–60 YEARS

DIG DEEP, BROTHERS- REMEMBER, Y'ALL ARE HELPING DO GOD'S WORK!
PIRAN
WHILE WE'RE COLLECTING THE LOVE OFFERING, LET ME SAY HOW HAPPY I AM THAT BROTHER SID INVITED ME TO BE CHAPLAIN OF THIS FINE ORGANIZATION!
PIRANHA CLUB
TAP TAP TAP
PIRANHA CLUB
©1988 King Features Syndicate, Inc. World rights reserved
THAT COLLECTION PLATE COST ME EIGHTEEN DOLLARS AND NINETY-FIVE CENTS!
6-10

MONK-EAZE® BRAND ANIMAL SERVANTS

TIRED OF HOUSEWORK?! WANT TO LIVE LIKE THE KENNEDYS?! ALWAYS WANTED YOUR OWN SERVANTS BUT COULDN'T AFFORD IT?!
© 1988 King Features Syndicate Inc World rights reserved
WELL, NOW YOU CAN WITH MONK-EAZE® BRAND ANIMAL SERVANTS! YES, MONK-EAZE MONKEYS COOK! CLEAN! WASH YOUR CLOTHES! THEY EVEN REPAIR YOUR CAR!
1-555-MONKEYS
...AND THESE AREN'T CHEAP, RUN-OF-THE-MILL MONKEYS! THEY'RE GENUINE, HARD-TO-GET SOUTH AMERICAN HOWLER MONKEYS! KNOWN FOR THEIR GENTLE DISPOSITION AND EAGERNESS TO PLEASE!
...I KNOW WHAT YOU'RE THINKING- "HOW MUCH DOES IT COST TO FEED THEM?" (HERE'S THE BEST PART...) THEY EAT GARBAGE!!
MY TROUBLES ARE OVER!
4-18
B. GRACE

IT'S HARD TO BELIEVE, BUT THIS CRATE IS FULL OF HIGHLY TRAINED MONK-EAZE® BRAND ANIMAL SERVANTS!
I GOT A MAID, A BUTLER, A CHEF...
© 1988 King Features Syndicate, Inc. World rights reserved
NO MORE HOUSEWORK FOR ME! WATCH THIS...
OK! WHO TAKES OUT THE GARBAGE? LET'S GO! TAKE OUT THE GARBAGE!
GARBAGE... TAKE OUT! TAKE-OUT-GARBAGE! GARBAGE-TAKE-OUT! TAKE-UH! OUT-UH! GARBAGE! TAKE! OUT!
TAKE OUT THE CENSORED GARBAGE! OK! WHICH ONE OF YOU IS THE MAID? TAKE-OUT-GARBAGE! DON'T EAT THE GARBAGE!
TAKE IT OUT!
4-19 B. GRACE

THE PROBLEM IS, THEY'RE STUPID - THEY DON'T UNDERSTAND ENGLISH! YOU HAVE TO TALK TO THEM IN SIGN LANGUAGE!
HIGHLY TRAINED MONK-EAZE® BRAND ANIMAL SERVANTS
THEY HAVE A VOCABULARY OF ABOUT 20 SIMPLE COMMANDS LIKE 'SWEEP FLOOR' OR 'WASH CLOTHES'... AFTER ALL, THEY'RE ONLY DUMB ANIMALS!
© 1988 King Features Syndicate, Inc. World rights reserved
ERNIE
SO TELL THE MAID TO TAKE OUT THE GARBAGE
HEY! GIMME A BREAK!
I CAN'T LEARN A BRAND NEW LANGUAGE OVER-NIGHT!
4-20

SIGN LANGUAGE BOOK
© 1988 King Features Syndicate, Inc. World rights reserved
-TAKE- -OUT- -GARBAGE-
HIGHLY TRAINED MONK-EAZE® BRAND ANIMAL SERVANT
THE GREAT SPECKLED WATER TURKEY SELLS ROWBOATS IN THE CRATERED FIELDS OF VERDUN
BoGRACE

I'M BREAKING IN MY COOK- HE'S A HIGHLY TRAINED MONK-EAZE® BRAND ANIMAL SERVANT, BUT HE'S NOT QUITE USED TO HIS NEW SURROUNDINGS
© 1988 King Features Syndicate, Inc. World rights reserved
EVEN HUMAN CHEFS FROM, SAY, MONGOLIA WOULD NEED SOME TIME TO GET USED TO A TOTALLY NEW ENVIRONMENT, AND PIERRE HERE IS ONLY A MONKEY
BOILED CARDBOARD?
IT'S GETTING BETTER- YESTERDAY HE USED TOO MUCH SALT
4-22 BOGRACE

YOU GOT A MONKEY FOR COOKING, ONE FOR CLEANING AND ONE FOR THE LAUNDRY?
YEAH. WANT TO TRY ONE?
I'LL TRY THE ONE FOR COOKING
SO, HOW WAS YOUR DINNER?
TERRIFIC! ESPECIALLY THE TAIL!
LOTS OF BONES, LIKE PIG'S FEET
YOU ATE PIERRE?!
TASTED LIKE CHICKEN
4-23
B. GRACE

YEAH! MY LANDLADY ATE MY CHEF...WELL, SURE I FEEL BAD ABOUT IT!... AT LEAST I HAVE ONE LESS MONKEY TO WORRY ABOUT
TUG TUG
...AND YOU CAN BET THERE'S NO WAY ON EARTH I'M GOING TO GET ANOTHER MONKEY TO TAKE HIS PLACE!
YANK YANK
© 1988 King Features Syndicate, Inc. World rights reserved
BABY
BoGRACE
4-25

THESE MONKEYS ARE DRIVING ME NUTS! AND AS IF THINGS WEREN'T BAD ENOUGH, CARRUTHERS HERE WENT AND GOT FIFI PREGNANT! WHAT AM I GOING TO DO?!
© 1988 King Features Syndicate, Inc. World rights reserved
ASK ABOUT OUR PRIME FLORIDA REAL ESTATE
BAIL BONDS AVAILABLE
NOTARY PUBLIC
FERNWILTER ESTATE JEWELRY
YOU'RE LICENSED TO MARRY MONKEYS?
I'M THE ONLY ORDAINED MONKEY PREACHER IN THE ENTIRE STATE OF NEW JERSEY
4-26
BoGRACE

THE VFW HALL IS CLEANER, BUT THE ELKS LODGE HAS MORE SEATS... THE WURLITZER WILL RUN 80 BUCKS...ANOTHER 45 FOR THE ORGANIST... FLOWERS... CATERER...
© 1988 King Features Syndicate, Inc. World rights reserved
YOU MUST BE CRAZY!
AS FATHER OF THE BRIDE, I WOULD HOPE YOU'D SETTLE FOR NOTHING BUT THE BEST!
WHAT FATHER OF THE BRIDE?! SHE'S A PREGNANT MONKEY!
SO SCRATCH THE CATERER - I'LL PICK UP A COUPLE DOZEN BANANAS
4-27

NOW, AS SOON AS THE MATRON OF HONOR FINISHES "O PROMISE ME," I'LL SAY "DEARLY BELOVED, WE ARE GATHERED ETC. ETC..."
© 1988 King Features Syndicate, Inc. World rights reserved
REMINDS ME OF MY MARRIAGE TO BRUNO
THEN COMES THE TRADITIONAL MONKEY MARRIAGE RITUAL
WHICH IS...
THEY PICK BUGS OFF EACH OTHER
4-28
REMINDS ME OF OUR HONEYMOON AT THE HOTEL CUCARACHA
B. GRACE

I'LL SAY, "WHO HAS COME TO GIVE THIS MONKEY AWAY?" THEN YOU'LL SAY, "I, HER FATHER"...
FOR THE LAST TIME... I HAVE NO DAUGHTER!
DON'T WORRY, HONEY— HE'LL CHANGE HIS MIND WHEN HE SEES HIS GRANDCHILD!
BOGRACE
4-29
© 1988 King Features Syndicate, Inc. World rights reserved

720 BUCKS MAY SEEM HIGH, BUT YOU GET A LOT OF EXTRA EXPENSE WITH A MONKEY MARRIAGE – TAIL HOLES IN THE TUXEDOS, SHEET MUSIC TO "ABBA DABBA DABBA"...
FORGET IT, UNCLE SID. THEY ELOPED LAST NIGHT.
B. GRACE
©1988 King Features Syndicate, Inc. World rights reserved
SO WHAT ARE YOU MOANING ABOUT?!
THEY TOOK MY CAR
4-30

SID'S TRIAL

I DECIDED I'M GOING TO HELP BEAUTIFY THE CITY!
YOU'RE MOVING TO ARIZONA?
I'M GOING TO HAVE SOMEONE PAINT A MURAL ON THE SIDE OF MY HOUSE!
TRUST ME, EFFIE! IT'S AS GOOD AS DONE!
© 1988 King Features Syndicate, Inc. World rights reserved
HONEST SID
FERNWILTER & CO. INVESTMENTS 555-1212
ASK ABOUT OUR PRIME FLORIDA REAL ESTATE
TRUST ME
5-2
BOGRACE

SIDNEY FERNWILTER— YOU ARE CHARGED WITH TWO HUNDRED EIGHTY COUNTS OF SOLICITING WITH INTENT TO DEFRAUD.
© 1988 King Features Syndicate, Inc. World rights reserved
...AND WHILE WE'RE AT IT, THERE'S ALSO A SMALL MATTER OF NINE UNPAID PARKING TICKETS!
HOW DO YOU PLEAD?
DO I HAVE A CHOICE?
OF COURSE, YOU HAVE A CHOICE
I'LL TAKE THE PARKING TICKETS
BGRACE
5-3

GEE, UNCLE SID- IS THERE ANYTHING I CAN DO TO HELP?
YEAH
TAKE THIS DEPOSIT OVER TO 'FRED'S BAIL BONDS' ON FOURTH STREET
5-4
BGRACE
SO WHAT ARE YOU IN FOR?
TRYING TO PASS A BAD CHECK
YEAH? ME TOO

THE JUDGE GAVE ME FIFTY HOURS OF COMMUNITY SERVICE. HE CALLED IT MY REHABILITATION PROGRAM
DON'T KNOCK IT, ERNIE! I KNOW A GUY–HE WAS A TWO-BIT CON ARTIST–WENT TO LAW SCHOOL IN PRISON...
NOW HE'S A LAWYER–HE PULLS DOWN HALF A MILLION A YEAR!
THANK GOD FOR CRIMINAL REHABILITATION
DARN RIGHT!
5-5
BGRACE

INTRODUCTIONS

WAIT TILL YOU MEET HIM! HE'S TALL AND GOOD-LOOKING AND VERY, VERY INTELLIGENT AND HE HAS A TERRIFIC SENSE OF HUMOR AND HE'S A GREAT CONVERSATIONALIST AND HE'S VERY POLITE AND CONSIDERATE ETC. ETC.
6-13
BOGRACE
ERNIE, THIS IS MY ROOMMATE, FELICIA LOPEZ
GRUNT
© 1988 King Features Syndicate Inc. World rights reserved
WHAT DO YOU THINK?
I THINK I LIKE **YOUR** VERSION BETTER
ITCH
ITCH

I THOUGHT YOU SAID HE LOOKS LIKE TOM SELLECK
HE HAS A MOUSTACHE
I THINK HE LOOKS MORE LIKE CLARK GABLE!
CLARK GABLE?! IN WHAT WAY?
6-14
HE LOOKS LIKE HE'S BEEN DEAD TWENTY-FIVE YEARS
B. GRACE
©1988 King Features Syndicate, Inc. World rights reserved

ALL KIDDING ASIDE, ERNIE—YOU'RE NOT SUCH A BAD-LOOKING GUY! LET'S SHAKE HANDS AND BE FRIENDS!
DORIS' ROOM-MATE, FELICIA
© 1988 King Features Syndicate, Inc. World rights reserved
COME ON!... SHAKE HANDS! SHAKE!
SHAKE!
COME ON, BOY! SHAKE HANDS!
6-15
GOOD BOY!
HAS HE BEEN WORMED AND HAD HIS SHOTS?
BGRACE

ERNIE LEARNED THE FAST-FOOD BUSINESS AT CAL TECH DIDN'T YOU, ERNIE?
CAL TECH? PERHAPS I MISJUDGED YOU
PERHAPS YOU DID
WHAT DID YOU MAJOR IN?
HAMBURGERS
HAM-BURGERS?
AFTER COW TECH I WENT TO POTATO TECH AND GOT A DEGREE IN FRENCH FRIES
BOGRACE 6-16
© 1988 King Features Syndicate Inc World rights reserved

ERNIE'S CRAZY ABOUT ME, BUT HE'S VERY STOIC! HE DOESN'T LET HIS FEELINGS SHOW!
OH HI, SWEETIE! WANT TO TAKE ME TO LUNCH?
I'D LOVE TO, BUT I'M LATE FOR A ROOT CANAL
Menu
SEE WHAT I MEAN! IF I WERE ON MY WAY TO A ROOT CANAL, I'D BE A NERVOUS WRECK!
Menu
B. GRACE 6-24

OK, FELICIA! TELL ME EXACTLY WHAT YOU THINK OF ERNIE!
MEETING ERNIE WAS LIKE EATING MY MOTHER'S BEAN AND CABBAGE SOUP - I WAS ABLE TO CHOKE IT DOWN BUT I'LL HAVE A STOMACH-ACH FOR THE NEXT WEEK
YOU'RE JEALOUS!
© 1988 King Features Syndicate, Inc. World rights reserved
BoGRACE 6·17

THE UTILITIES

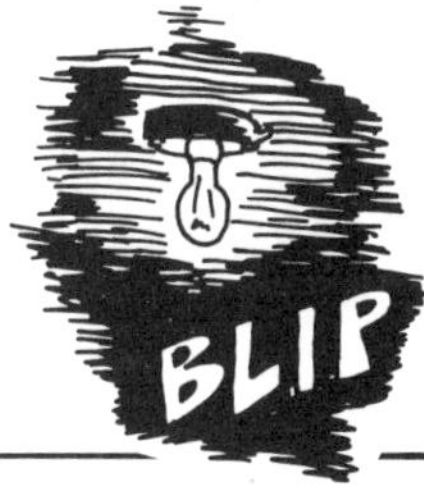
BLIP

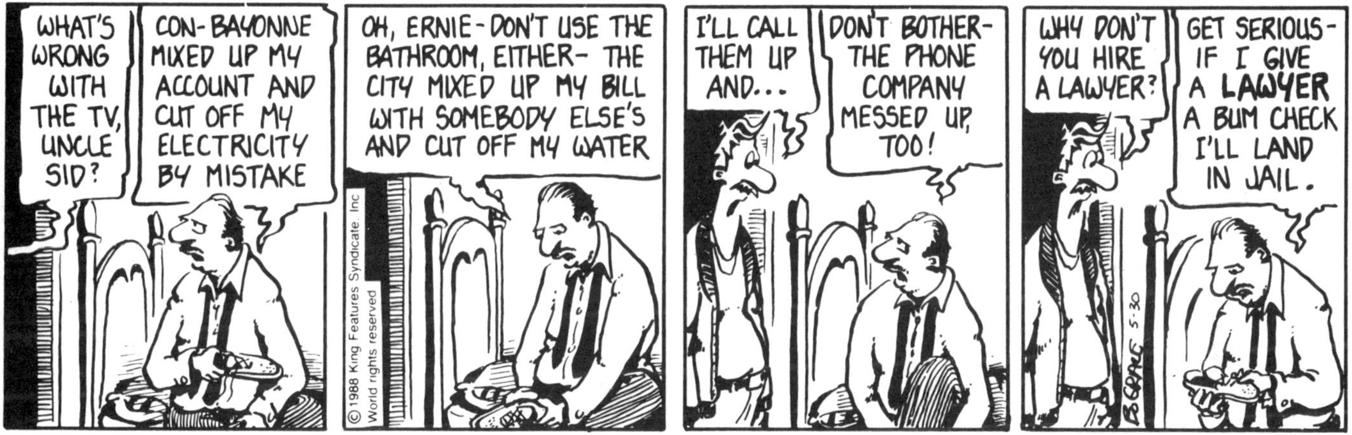
WHAT'S WRONG WITH THE TV, UNCLE SID?
CON-BAYONNE MIXED UP MY ACCOUNT AND CUT OFF MY ELECTRICITY BY MISTAKE
OH, ERNIE - DON'T USE THE BATHROOM, EITHER - THE CITY MIXED UP MY BILL WITH SOMEBODY ELSE'S AND CUT OFF MY WATER
© 1988 King Features Syndicate, Inc
World rights reserved
I'LL CALL THEM UP AND...
DON'T BOTHER - THE PHONE COMPANY MESSED UP, TOO!
WHY DON'T YOU HIRE A LAWYER?
GET SERIOUS - IF I GIVE A LAWYER A BUM CHECK I'LL LAND IN JAIL.
5-30

YOU SAY WE CUT OFF YOUR ELECTRICITY BY MISTAKE, MR. FERNWILTER?
YESSIR.
ACCORDING TO THIS, THE LAST TIME YOU PAID YOUR BILL WAS MAY, 1983!... WHAT WAS IT, MR. FERNWILTER?! WHAT WENT WRONG?!
MAY, 1983!... I WON THE DAILY DOUBLE, GOT LOADED AND FIGURED, HECK, I'LL PAY MY BILLS...
5-31
BUT BELIEVE ME, SIR! I HAVEN'T BEEN DRUNK LIKE THAT IN YEARS!
BOEDACE
© 1988 King Features Syndicate, Inc. World rights reserved

HI, FRED–I KNEW YOU WOULDN'T MIND IF I USED YOUR FAUCET TO WATER MY TOMATOES
AT TWO O'CLOCK IN THE MORNING?
YEAH! I LOVE TOMATOES, AND IT'S THE ONLY WAY TO GET THE BIG ONES!
THERE'S ANOTHER WAY TO GET BIG TOMATOES
HOW?
FIRST YOU PAY YOUR WATER BILL...
I LOVE 'EM– I DON'T WANT TO MARRY 'EM!
B.GRACE 6-1
© 1988 King Features Syndicate, Inc. World rights reserved

I SEE YOUR POWER IS BACK ON
I'D HAVE WATER, TOO, IF IT WASN'T FOR THAT CHEAPSKATE NEXT DOOR!
6-2
HOW COME?
THE OLD TIGHTWAD WOULDN'T LET ME PUT A HOSE ON HIS OUTSIDE FAUCET
BLIP
WHAT HAPPENED?
THE CHEAP
FOUND MY EXTENSION CORD!

HOW LONG HAS IT BEEN?
A MONTH
A MONTH SINCE THE CITY CUT OFF YOUR WATER AND ELECTRICITY?!
YEAH-AND **NEXT** MONTH I'M GETTING EVICTED FOR NOT PAYING MY RENT!
6-3
12 DONUTS
AREN'T YOU WORRIED?
YOU BET I'M WORRIED!
©1988 King Features Syndicate, Inc. World rights reserved
I THINK I'M LOSING MY TIMING
12 DONUTS
BOGRACE

FACE IT, UNCLE SID– THERE'S NO WAY THE CITY WILL TURN YOUR UTILITIES BACK ON!
REALLY, ERNIE?
ABSOLUTELY NOT! NOT WHILE YOU HAVE SUCH LOUSY CREDIT!
NO KIDDING!
AND THE ONLY WAY TO GET GOOD CREDIT IS TO ALWAYS PAY YOUR BILLS ON TIME!
YOU DON'T SAY!
YOUR NAME?
ERNIE FLOYD
-UTILITIES-
NEW ACCOUNTS
12 DONUTS
6-4
BGRACE

THE NOSE JOB

THERE'S LOUIE! HE'S SO SENSITIVE ABOUT HIS APPEARANCE! TRY TO SAY SOMETHING NICE!
RELAX! I WAS FOUR YEARS AT DALE CARNEGIE!
HELLO, ERNIE
HI! WHAT'S UP?
HELLO, SID
I BEG YOUR PARDON
IT'S ME—LOUIE!
OH, SORRY, LOUIE! I DIDN'T RECOGNIZE YOU WITH THE HAT!
9-22 BGRACE

I'VE DECIDED! I'M GETTING A NOSE JOB!
NO KIDDING, LOUIE ?! HOW COME?
FOR ONE THING, IT'S HARD TO MEET GIRLS
HELLO, BIG BOY! GOT A LIGHT?
WHAM!
SEE WHAT I MEAN?
© 1988 King Features Syndicate, Inc. World rights reserved
9-23 B. GRACE

IF YOU'RE THINKING OF SURGERY, GIVE MY PAL A CALL – HE'S THE BEST NOSE DOCTOR AROUND! HE'LL TURN THAT WURLITZER INTO A STRADIVARIUS!
TRUST ME, LOUIE! THIS GUY WILL MAKE YOU LOOK LIKE A **MOVIE STAR**!
LASSIE
619
ENOS PORK. MD
Eyes, Ears Nose and Throat
Brain Surgery by Appointment
The Doctor is IN
9-24
BGRACE
© 1988 King Features Syndicate, Inc. World rights reserved

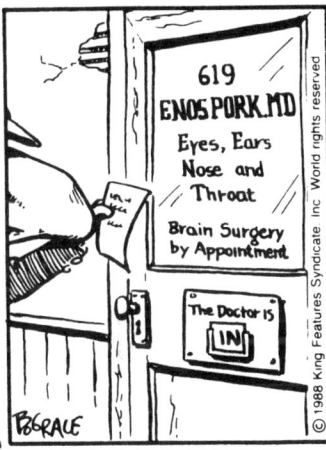

THIS IS LOUIS PITTS, DOCTOR—MR. PITTS WANTS...
DON'T TELL ME! LET ME GUESS!
ENOS PORK, MD
HYPEREXTENDED NECK MUSCLES?
WHIPLASH FROM SNEEZING?
ENOS PORK, MD
9-26
BOGRACE
© 1988 King Features Syndicate Inc. World rights reserved
YOUR MONOGRAMMED SHEETS DON'T FIT IN THE BREAST POCKET OF YOUR SUIT!
MOSS GROWS ON YOUR UPPER LIP!
ENOS PORK, MD
YOUR BACK HURTS FROM PICKING UP PEANUTS!
YOU'RE GOING BROKE BUYING FURNITURE POLISH!!
YOU'RE ALLERGIC TO BAT FUR!!

THE REASON I'VE COME TO SEE YOU, DR. PORK, IS BECAUSE I'M CONSIDERING COSMETIC SURGERY
ENOS PORK, MD
ENOS PORK, MD
JUST THE NOSE, OR DO YOU WANT ME TO TAKE CARE OF THE STRETCH MARKS ON YOUR FOREHEAD?
ENOS PORK, MD
9-27 BGRACE
©1988 King Features Syndicate, Inc. World rights reserved

HOW MUCH IS MY NOSE JOB GOING TO COST, DR. PORK
ENOS PORK, MD
LIKE ALL REPUTABLE SURGEONS I CHARGE BY THE POUND...
ENOS PORK, MD
© 1988 King Features Syndicate, Inc. World rights reserved
PLUS, OF COURSE, THE USUAL INCIDENTAL EXPENSES...
ENOS PORK, MD.
SEAT COVERS FOR THE BMW
ANESTHESIA, $450
COUNTRY CLUB DUES
HEMOSTATS, $750
BOOKIE
SPONGES, $2657...
ENOS PORK, MD
9-28
BGRACE

GEE... ISN'T THERE SOME WAY WE COULD CUT THE COST?
WELL, WE COULD ALWAYS TRY IT WITHOUT ANESTHESIA
ENOS PORK, MD
WON'T THAT HURT?
EVERYBODY HAS A DIFFERENT PAIN THRESHOLD, IT ALL DEPENDS ON YOUR BASAL METABOLISM- I'LL BE GLAD TO TEST YOURS
OK.
PORK, MD
PSSSSSS
YAAA!
ARE WE READY TO STOP DICKERING?
GGGGG
BREATHED 9-29
© 1988 King Features Syndicate, Inc. World rights reserved

RELAX AND COUNT BACKWARDS FROM A HUNDRED, LOUIE- AND DON'T WORRY!
REMEMBER, I'M NOT JUST YOUR SURGEON, I'M YOUR FRIEND!
GREETINGS FROM THE WORLD'S BIGGEST
ZZZZZZ
10-1
BGRACE
© 1988 King Features Syndicate, Inc. World rights reserved

TA-DAHHH!
© 1988 King Features Syndicate, Inc. World rights reserved
IT'S ME... LOUIE! I GOT MY NOSE JOB!
YOU LOOK LIKE JACK NICHOLSON
YES, SIR! HE SURE DID A GREAT JOB FIXING MY NOSE!
10-3
WHAT'S THIS? SNIFF? SNIFF? SMELLS GOOD! SNIFF?
LAST MONTH'S GUACAMOLE
BOGRAD

SO, LOUIE - YOU DECIDED TO GO TO UNCLE SID'S DOCTOR FOR YOUR NOSE JOB!
IT WAS HARD TO TURN HIM DOWN ONCE HE THREW IN THE FREE BONUS GIFT!
I COULD HAVE HAD A PEN-AND-PENCIL SET OR A TOASTER OR A SLIDE RULE, BUT I TOOK THE GENUINE LEATHER CUSTOM-MADE EXECUTIVE ATTACHÉ CASE!
BGRACE
10-4
© 1988 King Features Syndicate Inc World rights reserved

EVERYBODY LOOKS AT ME NOW WHEN I GO TO WORK! I DON'T KNOW IF IT'S MY NOSE JOB OR MY CLASSY NEW BRIEFCASE!
HOW DO YOU OPEN IT?
I'M SURE IT'S A GUCCI, BUT I CAN'T FIND THE LABEL
10-5
BGRACE

NOW WHERE DID I PUT THAT?...
DID YOU LOSE YOUR PAPERS?
HECK NO! I'M LOOKING FOR MY LUNCH!
WANT A SANDWICH?
NO THANKEW
BOGRACE
10-6
© 1988 King Features Syndicate, Inc. World rights reserved

PASS THE PEPPER, PLEASE
BOGRACE
ONE THING LIVERWURST NEEDS IS PEPPER!
LOTS OF PEPPER
© 1988 King Features Syndicate, Inc. World rights reserved
KABOOM!
THE LAST THING I REMEMBER HIS SUITCASE BLEW UP
10-7

OH, ERNIE! MY POOR ERNIE! OH, ERNIE ERNIE ERNIE ERNIE ERNIE ERNIE ERNIE ERNIE ERNIE!
I'LL STAY WITH YOU, ERNIE! I'LL BE WITH YOU NIGHT AND DAY! I WON'T LEAVE YOUR SIDE TILL YOUR POOR BROKEN BODY IS HEALED!
DOESN'T IT HURT TO WALK ON THOSE BROKEN BONES?
BoGRACE
10-8

DATING

BARREL O' CORN

C'MON!
WOULD YOU SEE WHAT'S TAKING DORIS SO LONG?!
MAYBE SHE DROWNED IN THE SINK...
I SHOULD BE SO LUCKY!
© 1988 King Features Syndicate, Inc. World rights reserved
DO YOU THINK I SHOULD CHANGE MY DRESS?
YES—AND WHILE YOU'RE AT IT, WASH AND SET YOUR HAIR
8-2 BERRACE

SO WHAT HAPPENED TO **YOUR** DATE TONIGHT, FELICIA?
HE HAD TO PERFORM EMERGENCY BYPASS SURGERY ON THE PRIME MINISTER OF YUGOSLAVIA
WHAT HAPPENED TO FELICIA'S DATE TONIGHT?
SHE GOT STOOD UP
8-3
BGRACE

FELICIA- WHY DON'T YOU LIKE ERNIE?
BECAUSE HE'S A JERK.
© 1988 King Features Syndicate, Inc. World rights reserved
ERNIE- WHY DON'T YOU LIKE FELICIA?
BECAUSE SHE'S A JERK!
BARREL O' CORN
8-4
I DON'T UNDERSTAND WHY THEY DON'T GET ALONG- THEY HAVE SO MUCH IN COMMON!

YOU'RE NOT A BAD-LOOKING WOMAN, FELICIA! WHY DON'T WE GET TOGETHER FOR A DRINK AND A GOOD TIME?
FINE BY ME! BUT IT'S GOT TO BE OUT OF TOWN! CAN YOU BE AT THE HOTEL LA BOMBA BAR IN PHILADELPHIA AT 8 O'CLOCK TONIGHT?
IT'LL TAKE ME HALF THE DAY TO GET TO PHILLY!
BUT YOU'LL HAVE A NIGHT YOU'LL NEVER FORGET!
DRINK UP, MAC! I GOT TO CLOSE!
LA BOMB
BoGRACE 8-5

THE BEACH

IT'S AWFULLY SMALL
HONEY, IF YOU WANT TO CATCH A FISH YOU GOT TO BUY THE RIGHT BAIT!
SHARK BAIT?
BUT TOO MUCH LEAD IN HER SINKER!
9-5
B.GRACE

AREN'T YOU GOING TO TAKE OFF YOUR BEACH ROBE?
BGRACE
© 1988 King Features Syndicate, Inc. World rights reserved
I'M NOT USED TO A STRING BIKINI. IT'S THE FIRST TIME I EVER WORE ONE
THE TOP SEEMED SO MUCH BIGGER WHEN I PUT IT ON AT THE STORE
MAYBE AT THE STORE YOU DIDN'T PUT IT ON BACKWARDS
9-6

HEY, BABY! CHECK OUT THESE DELTS!
GO AWAY
SEE THAT MUSCLE? I CAN BENCH PRESS 200 POUNDS WITH MY EARS!
YOU BETTER LEAVE! MY BOYFRIEND WILL BE BACK ANY SECOND!
GOOD! I CAN USE THE PROTEIN!
HE'S GOING TO TEAR YOU LIMB FROM LIMB!
BOUNCE
BOUNCE
PIZZA! MAYBE SHE'D RATHER HAVE PIZZA! IT ONLY TAKES 20 OR 30 MINUTES!
9-7
BOGRACC
© 1988 King Features Syndicate, Inc. World rights reserved

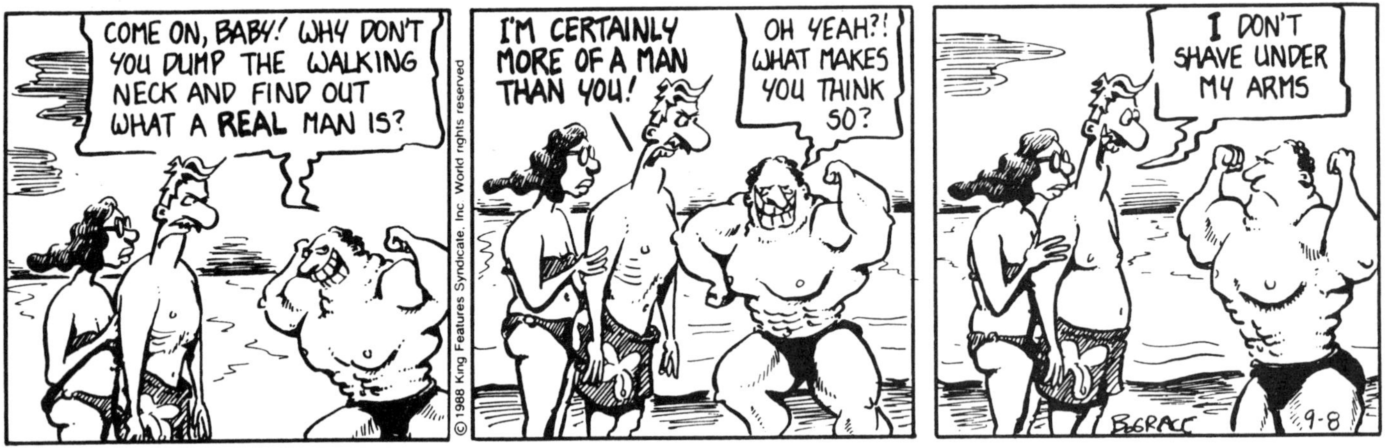
COME ON, BABY! WHY DON'T YOU DUMP THE WALKING NECK AND FIND OUT WHAT A **REAL** MAN IS?
I'M CERTAINLY MORE OF A MAN THAN YOU!
OH YEAH?! WHAT MAKES YOU THINK SO?
I DON'T SHAVE UNDER MY ARMS
BOGRACC
9-8

LOOK, MAC! THE LADY SAYS YOU'RE BUGGING HER! WHY DON'T YOU BEAT IT?!
OH YEAH?! WHO'S GOING TO MAKE ME?!
ME, THAT'S WHO!
HOW WAS THE BEACH?
WONDERFUL!
HOW WAS THE BEACH?
9-9
BOGRACE
© 1988 King Features Syndicate, Inc. World rights reserved

I JUST DON'T UNDERSTAND. YOU WENT TO THE BEACH WITH DORIS HUSSELMEYER, WHO YOU DON'T LIKE MUCH IN THE FIRST PLACE...
SOME 300-POUND NEANDERTHAL TRIES TO HIT ON HER – YOU COME TO HER RESCUE AND GET POUNDED!
AM I MISSING SOMETHING?
© 1988 King Features Syndicate, Inc. World rights reserved
A HEART?

HENSLOW

CAN I BORROW YOUR LAWN MOWER, HENSLOW?
GEE, I'D LOVE TO LET YOU HAVE IT, SID, BUT REMEMBER WHAT HAPPENED TO IT LAST TIME YOU BORROWED IT?
THAT WAS AN ACCIDENT! IT COULD'VE HAPPENED TO ANYBODY!
SO WHAT HAPPENED TO HIS MOWER LAST TIME?
I PAWNED IT
© 1988 King Features Syndicate, Inc World rights reserved

THAT HENSLOW BURNS ME UP! MY NEXT-DOOR NEIGHBOR AND HE WON'T LET ME BORROW HIS LAWN MOWER!
I ASK HIM VERY POLITELY– 'CAN I BORROW YOUR MOWER?' AND HE TURNS ME DOWN!
WHAT ARE NEIGHBORS FOR, FER CRYING OUT LOUD?!
BUT, UNCLE SID– YOU DON'T HAVE ANY GRASS
IT'S THE PRINCIPLE
BO GRACE
10-19
© 1988 King Features Syndicate Inc World rights reserved

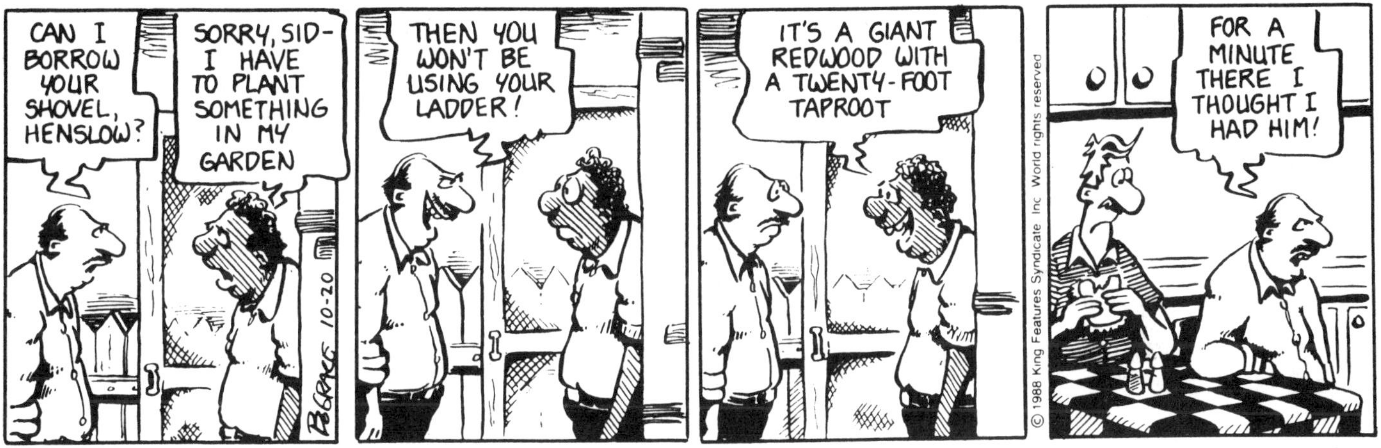
CAN I BORROW YOUR SHOVEL, HENSLOW?
SORRY, SID-I HAVE TO PLANT SOMETHING IN MY GARDEN
BGRACE 10-20
THEN YOU WON'T BE USING YOUR LADDER!
IT'S A GIANT REDWOOD WITH A TWENTY-FOOT TAPROOT
FOR A MINUTE THERE I THOUGHT I HAD HIM!
© 1988 King Features Syndicate Inc World rights reserved

HEY, HENSLOW-
CAN I BORROW
YOUR ACCORDIAN?
I DON'T
OWN AN
ACCORDIAN!
WHAT ARE
YOU SO
HAPPY
ABOUT?
I FINALLY
GOT A
DRAW!
10-21
B. GRACE

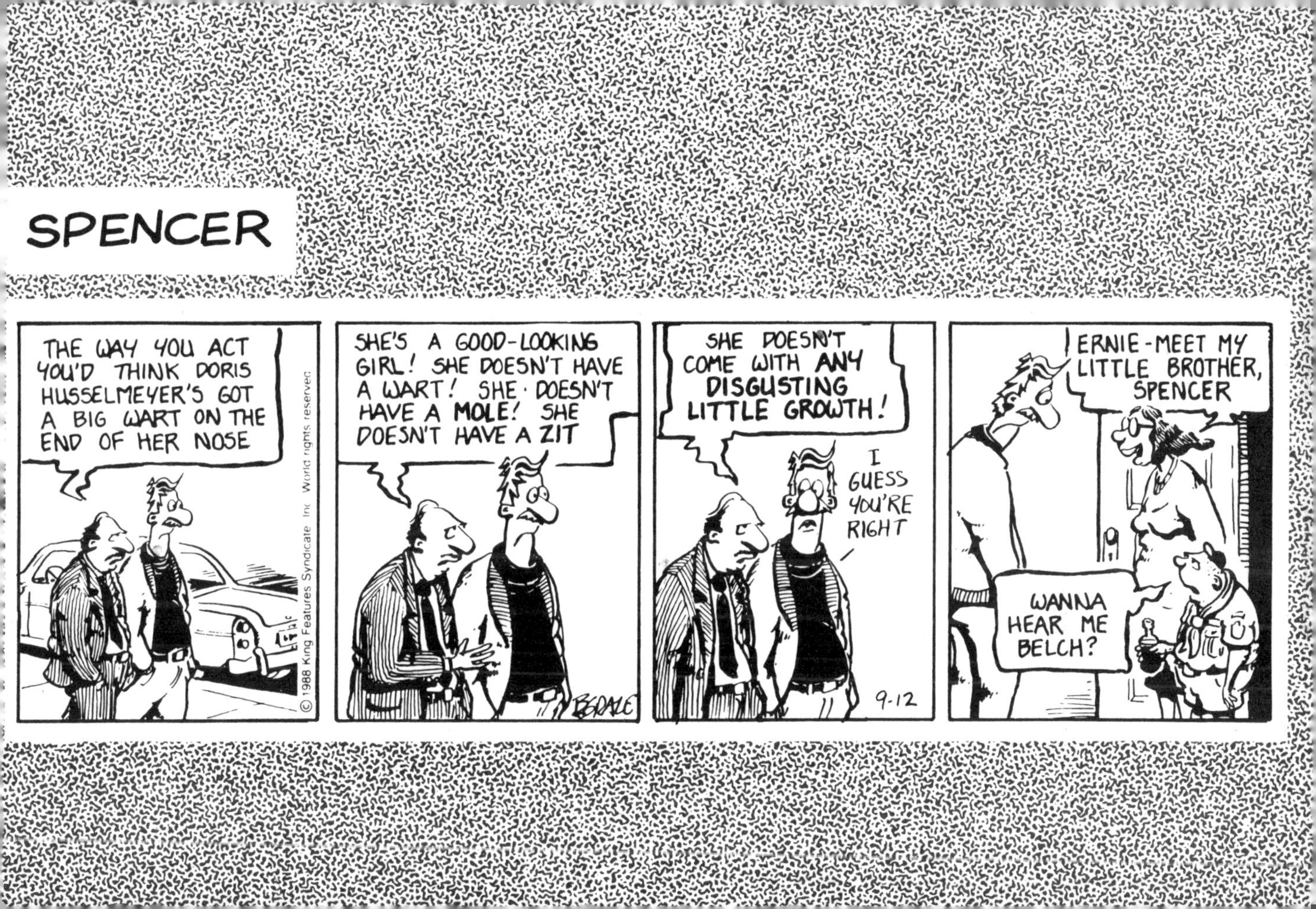
SPENCER
THE WAY YOU ACT YOU'D THINK DORIS HUSSELMEYER'S GOT A BIG WART ON THE END OF HER NOSE
© 1988 King Features Syndicate Inc World rights reserved
SHE'S A GOOD-LOOKING GIRL! SHE DOESN'T HAVE A WART! SHE DOESN'T HAVE A MOLE! SHE DOESN'T HAVE A ZIT
SHE DOESN'T COME WITH ANY DISGUSTING LITTLE GROWTH!
I GUESS YOU'RE RIGHT
9-12
ERNIE-MEET MY LITTLE BROTHER, SPENCER
WANNA HEAR ME BELCH?

MY PARENT'S HOUSE BURNED DOWN SO MY LITTLE BROTHER IS STAYING WITH ME FOR A WHILE
HIS HOUSE BURNED DOWN! POOR KID!
BGRACE
HI, SPENCER! WHADDAYA KNOW?!
9-13
I SURE AS HECK KNOW HOW TO RUB TWO STICKS TOGETHER
© 1988 King Features Syndicate Inc World rights reserved

SPENCER, YOU HAVE TO PUT YOUR TERRIBLE FEELINGS OF GUILT OUT OF YOUR MIND! STOP TORTURING YOURSELF!
BURNING DOWN YOUR MOMMY'S HOUSE WAS AN ACCIDENT! YOU CAN'T LET IT RUIN THE REST OF YOUR LIFE!
DORIS'S BROTHER
FOR GOD'S SAKE! DON'T LET THIS HORRIBLE TRAGEDY LEAVE A LIFELONG PSYCHOLOGICAL SCAR!
OK
CAN I HAVE A DOLLAR?
BOORACE 9-14

I THINK YOUR LITTLE BROTHER IS SUPPRESSING HIS DEEP FEELINGS OF GUILT FOR BURNING DOWN YOUR PARENTS' HOUSE...
HE NEEDS A HOBBY! SOMETHING TO KEEP HIS MIND OFF THE FIRE!
THANK GOODNESS FOR THE CUB SCOUTS!
I DON'T GET A CAMPFIRE MERIT BADGE?! WHAT DO I GOTTA DO? BURN DOWN THE WHOLE CITY?!
9-15
BOGRACE

BASIL

WHAT'S WRONG THIS TIME?
DORIS AND I ARE GOING ON A DOUBLE DATE WITH HER ROOMMATE
THERE'S NOBODY IN THE ENTIRE WORLD RUDER OR MORE INSENSITIVE THAN FELICIA!
© 1988 King Features Syndicate Inc World rights reserved
WHAT COULD BE WORSE THAN AN EVENING WITH FELICIA LOPEZ?!
BASIL, THIS IS ERNIE
IS THAT YOUR NOSE OR ARE YOU SUCKING A ZUCCHINI?

SORRY, FOLKS – I ONLY HAVE ROOM FOR THREE
TAXI
RATES
TOO BAD, FELICIA! IT LOOKS LIKE OUR DOUBLE DATE IS OFF
DON'T BE SILLY, ERNIE! BASIL WILL THINK OF SOMETHING!
TAXI
10-25
B.GRACE
© 1988 King Features Syndicate, Inc. World rights reserved
ARE YOU SURE HE CAN BREATHE?
MMMNF

HOW WAS YOUR DAY AT WORK, ERNIE?
SO-SO! THE SQUID BURGERS TURNED OUT TOUGH, BUT THE FRIES WEREN'T AS GREASY AS THEY USUALLY ARE!
I KNOW WHAT YOU MEAN! I HAD EXACTLY THE SAME KIND OF DAY!
MY MAHLER SOLO WAS TENTATIVE, BUT MY MOZART OBBLIGATO WAS SUPERB!
©1988 King Features Syndicate, Inc
World rights reserved
BUD GRACE 10-28

TELL ME, ERNIE - HOW DID YOU EVER BECOME INVOLVED WITH A GEEK LIKE DORIS?
11-1
© 1988 King Features Syndicate, Inc. World rights reserved
WHAT'S WRONG WITH BASIL?
HE ATE SOMETHING THAT DIDN'T AGREE WITH HIM
AK AK AK
OYSTERS?
TABLECLOTH
AK AK AK